THE DOORWAY PRINCE

A WELLS OF THE ONESONG STORY

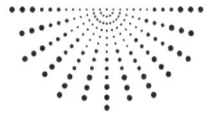

DAWN BLAIR

MORNING SKY STUDIOS

Ninjas

By the Numbers

Space Ninjas Aren't Real

Other stories

The Last Ant

Broken Smiles

Oxygen

I'm With Cupid

Let's Make a Deal

Nonfiction

The Write Edit

Children's Picture Books

Eggs at Play

THE DOORWAY PRINCE

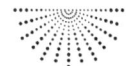

A faint, damp smell of rain came through the open window, making Eclipse look up from his desk. The sun still shone brightly in the sky, but he saw the droplets falling outside and could just barely make out the edges of a gray cloud which must be situated above the castle. The large leaves of the trees several yards from his window collected the water and dipped in the breeze. A servant boy pulling a cart full of tools hurried for the nearby livestock sheds. Eclipse couldn't help his chuckle as the boy walked beneath a branch that tipped its leaves over his head at that moment and drenched him. Some days were just like that.

Eclipse knew his day was coming.

He rose from his desk and crossed the room to his bookshelf. It had been awhile since Eclipse had allowed someone in here to clean; he couldn't afford to let anyone's energies conflict with his own while he made the necessary calculations. Dust piled on top of the wooden shelves, except in front of this one book which had a sharp-edged and dirtless track in front of it. Once again, he pulled the compendium smoothly from the shelf to consult with it as he had countless times already.

Eclipse just never liked the answer it kept giving him.

This time would be no different, he was certain. Yet he took it back to his desk and his calculations. He sat in the high-backed wooden chair once more, then put the book down atop his newest notes, lay his hands on the book, and blinked down his third lid. "Novestri ali'ack suventay."

The book began to vibrate beneath his palms. He held it down, violently willing this attempt to yield the answer he sought.

Rain pelted the window and Eclipse noticed the wind had kicked up. The approaching storm was blowing in earnest now, brewing overhead.

"I know," he whispered to the energy of the growing tempest. "Send me a good result this time."

As the book settled, he removed his hands from the leather cover. The text flipped open and rolled through the pages. At first, the paper was blank, but then ink rose to the surface, bleeding through the white surface until it was covered with odd scrolls, lines, and dots. Eclipse knew better than to try to interpret it until it was done. The Humline rarely answered in a linear fashion.

Once the page was filled from top to bottom, Eclipse set to deciphering the writing. The first thing he noticed was the spiral pattern to it. He still wouldn't get a straight answer. Even the spiral had waves to the lines and some letters and words were written larger than others.

CalcUlations, calcuLATIONS, Eclipse! Be Brave. yoU have the Answer You seek. Why keep asking? Questions, QUESTions, Eclipse. be NOT blind. Let the SON come forth. Do not hide IT behind youR cloak. Let the POWER not be ECLIPSED. Seek in the city and there you shall find HIM. Star 5402, Venric ipSON, DO NOT believe YOUR DOOM.

He slammed the book closed and paused for only a moment while he took a couple angry breaths. Maybe he was getting too old to be listening to the Humline. Then, swiftly, gracefully, he moved the book from atop his notes back to the shelf. Again.

"Cazidor," he muttered, pointing his hand at the desk. His notes lit on fire and burned quickly upon the polished wood until only a pile of ash remained. He needed to look at the stars, but there would be none with this storm.

Eclipse had just removed his black robes, leaving him in a ruffled white shirt and black pants, when a soft knock came to the door.

Eclipse thought about telling the sapere to enter, then thought against it. Instead, he thundered to the door and threw it open himself.

Sapere Palion stepped back, staring up at Eclipse's fuming countenance and Eclipse realized that he hadn't yet blinked back the dragonlids. He saw Palion with a white aura around him. The tattoos on the sapere's shaven head sparkled with golden flecks of the dragon magic bequeathed upon him. Palion's robes were also black, though not nearly as heavy as the cloak Eclipse had been wearing.

"I'm sorry to disturb you," Palion said. "Regent Sassio wants to know if you've had any luck. The Outliers are getting restless."

"I will bring them news when I have it," Eclipse growled. He stepped forward, making the sapere step back out of Eclipse's way. "I must go seek the city again."

"It will be getting dark soon," the sapere hesitated.

"The Humline cares not for time. Only that its will is met." Eclipse continued on through the halls and exited the castle. He stretched his shirt off over his head with an easy, practiced shrug and tucked it into the waistband of his pants. Once on the cobblestone path that led up to the castle, Eclipse extended his dragon wings and took to the sky. He loosened his long hair, letting the wind batter it around his face. If the Humline wanted a dark demon, so be it. A prince needed to be found and soon. If Eclipse could not deliver the next ruler of the realm, then he would have to fight to defend the reigning territory from invaders.

If only King Henoldis had not left this world without leaving behind an heir.

Eclipse soared through the moist, opaque clouds and felt the electricity build within the sky. It sparkled with snapping static along his skin. The churning currents buffeted against his wings and threatened a couple of times to send him spiraling. He demanded more and his wings responded with strong thrusts that sent him higher.

The clouds eased back and the blue sky above filled with bright sunlight. The sun already sat near the horizon. Soon it would set and leave him in darkness. Who knew what manner of creatures would come out of the blackness tonight?

But if the Humline was correct, the next ruler of the land would be out in the cold night as well. As a novihomidrak, very little could endanger or harm Eclipse, but the same could not be said for the unknown prince.

Star 5402, the Humline had told him. It hadn't been the first time that the Humline had given him that clue as to how to find the prince and Eclipse had been tracking the star's path through the night sky for many months now. So well he knew its path now that he could calculate where it would be during the day as well as finding it in an instant at night. It would rise soon after nightfall.

But how would the star help him to find a prince among the masses in the city?

Calzel, the local people called the star. Technically, it wasn't one star either, but rather overlapping stars which looked like a single bright star instead of two. It made up part of the Hunter constellation, the very center of the Hunter's bow where it was said that the Hunter released an arrow and killed the Grekish, a terrible monster of the land. But Eclipse knew more of the story than the locals did. Their Hunter was actually a novihomidrak called Moonhunter and his bow called Tranquility. Did this mean that the prince the Onesong was sending him was actually a novihomidrak? Is that why Eclipse personally resisted this mission, because he knew that only by another novihomidrak could he find death, something he wasn't quite sure he was ready for?

Eclipse flew toward the city, breathing deeply of the thin, charged air as the sun set behind him and the last rays of day began to fade. Back down through the storm he went.

Would tonight be the time when he'd discover the signs the Humline had been sending to him through his calculations and dreams? Would he be able to pull back the veil to see what mechanics were really working behind the scenes?

Rain came straight down on him, running in cold torrents off his black wings. Below the clouds, the land was bathed in the rainstorm's grayness. The streets of the city were nearly empty as people hurried home before total darkness claimed the land. Without even a solitary moon, the nights on this planet were truly black, yet the stars so clear that it was no wonder the people of Pillath told stories about them. If only they understood that the monsters of the universe were drawn to Pillath because of the dark cover of night too. Novihomidraks had been sent to this planet so often they had been put in charge of finding rulers for the land. Now not only did the novihomidraks have to be saviors, but oracles as well. Oh well, Eclipse thought to himself. It wasn't the first time and he was certain it wasn't the last. He was one of a rare few that could actually make a difference in a world's ill-fated history.

Eclipse landed on the dirt street, his boots splashing up droplets of mud onto his pants. His wings shrunk and tucked back under his skin as he took his wet shirt from his waistband and put it on. For a moment, he wished he'd thought to grab a cloak. Though he knew he could call one to him, it would be soaked in a matter of moments anyway, so what was the point?

The shutters of the buildings all around him were closed, most having cloth pulled down behind them as well to protect from the wind that might try to blow through them and to hide the light of candles and lanterns inside.

On most worlds Eclipse had come to before being assigned here, the small stretch between the sand colored buildings would be called an alleyway rather than a street. But the people of Pillath had yet to develop transportation beyond small wagons. Most vehicles were carts at best. Maybe it had to do with the lack of large loadbearing animals on this world. There were no horses or oxen. Most anything larger than a dog was not something one wanted to encounter. Carnivorous and lethal were understated qualities of the creatures here.

A howl rose in the distance barely outside the city walls and Eclipse turned to listen. So a frekisbeast thought it would hunt tonight, did it? Not near his city. Eclipse took a deep breath and bent over with his hands on his knees as he screamed out in rage. He felt the dragonlids come down, sharpening his vision, as if preparing for a real attack. Claws grew from his fingertips. For a second, Eclipse nearly lost control under the primal power he sent through himself and he had to stop himself from going out to destroy the frekisbeast. He would deal with it later.

Swallowing back the rush of saliva which entered his mouth and licking the spit that had escaped onto his lips, Eclipse stood and tried to calm his heartbeat.

"You are a dark demon?" a small voice said behind him.

Eclipse whirled at the sound, claws out and ready for an attack, his dragon teeth baring.

His dragon vision caught sight of a preteen boy with a blue aura curled tightly in a doorway. The stench that rose from him made Eclipse wonder why his novihomidrak senses hadn't picked up the youngster earlier. How could it be that the rain hadn't washed that smell from him? Eclipse turned his head away and snarled while still watching the boy in his peripheral vision.

"I've watched you go down this street several times," the boy said. "What are you looking for?"

Eclipse wanted to speak, but the odor of stale dirt rankled in his nose. He stumbled backwards, careful to not stop looking at the street rat. "You've seen me?"

"I just told you that," the boy answered. He stretched out his long legs, turning so he was casually sitting on the top step. His pants were filthy and ripped while his tunic was threadbare and had tattered holes in several places. He wore no shoes and by the looks of the blackened bottoms of his feet he never had. Meals seemed to be another thing that didn't come often to him. While he didn't have the gaunt look of a starved child, he was as slim as his skeleton. Eclipse wondered if the boy's skin was as worn in places as was his clothes. Maybe festering wounds accounted for the rotten stink. "You're the prophet from the castle, aren't you?"

Eclipse took a careful step back, disliking the earthy taste that entered his mouth as if he'd swallowed a pile of dirt pissed on by rats. His dragon senses wouldn't quit either. What about this boy kept Eclipse in a state of alarm? "I am."

"So, why are you here? To be down here, especially in the rain, you must be looking for something. Whatcha looking for?" the boy repeated.

"An arrow," Eclipse responded.

"That's an odd thing to be looking for in a storm. Aren't you a novihomidrak? What would one of the dragon born be doing out here looking for an arrow?" The boy stood with a graceful ease which unnerved Eclipse and made him jump backwards.

"Easy now," said the boy. "I ain't wanting no trouble. I'm going to go and let you look for your arrow. All right?" The kid stepped off the short staircase and glided along the building's wall, keeping his back to it so he could watch Eclipse. He slid out into the street, nearly slipping in the mud.

Eclipse saw it, the sign. Through the break in the clouds, a star shone brightly over the boy's head. Star 5402. Eclipse stretched out his hand toward the boy. "Wait," he called out, the word coming as a dragon whisper between his extended teeth.

The boy froze.

"What is your name?" Eclipse asked, a sizzle of magic running over the words.

"I have none," the boy responded.

Bathed under the pinpoint of light by the Star 5402, the boy's aura shifted to a golden white. Only then did Eclipse notice that the rain had stopped.

"You have no parents. Do you know from where you come?" Eclipse asked.

The boy started a slow shake of his head. "Please don't eat me."

Those words took Eclipse back. "Why would you think that I would eat you? You smell worse than the stockyard's manure pits."

The boy turned and ran.

Star 5402 slipped behind a cloud.

Eclipse sighed. His dragon reflexes relaxed, the claws and teeth retracting, the dragonlids lifting. What good would it do to have a king that riled him so? Eclipse didn't know, but he had to go after the boy. Following his nose, Eclipse took to the hunt.

When Eclipse reached the intersection, the streets were empty. Already the boy's scent was beginning to fade to the musty dampness of the rainstorm and the cleansing breeze. But the same could not be said for the preteen's tracks. They read clearly in the mud, deep impressions of the fronts of his feet and his toes meaning he was pushing off hard with each step. Life on the streets had taught him how to run fast.

"Why a street urchin?" Eclipse growled as if he could ask the Onesong that very question and get a reply. Most likely, the kid had stolen the clothes he had on and any decent meal he ever ate when he couldn't scrounge enough scraps to eat. The Onesong just expected Eclipse to pick the boy up and pluck him down on the throne to the kingdom. If Eclipse were lucky, the kid wouldn't bolt with all the gold and silver his scrawny body could carry until the second night.

Eclipse followed the tracks until they disappeared. Literally, there in the middle of the street, the footprints in the mud just vanished. Eclipse looked up and saw a rope crossing between two buildings. Eclipse glanced back at the tracks and saw that the distance between steps had shortened as the boy quickened for a jump. Here, in the near pitch black of oncoming night, the kid had known the rope was there. He knew the streets well enough to find his way in the dark. Eclipse brought down the dragonlids and searched the buildings for any signs of the boy. The rope was still hot, most likely from crossing his legs around the rope as he climbed fast. He then had used a ledge to climb up on the building. Eclipse caught a glimpse of the boy hoisting himself over the side and rolling onto the roof.

Eclipse removed his shirt and extended his dragon wings. He flew up to the rooftop where the boy was currently launching himself between buildings. The boy tucked and rolled as he made a near effortless landing.

The practiced ease had the kid up and running for the next building in mere seconds.

Eclipse sighed again. "Here we go," he whispered, then took flight after the boy. Eclipse swooped the kid up as he jumped between buildings again. The boy's arms and legs scrambled beneath him as he realized he'd been caught.

"Help!" the kid screamed. "The demon's got me."

"Mezzipalor," Eclipse said. The boy went limp in his arms. Then to the sleeping prince, Eclipse whispered, "For the record, I'm not a demon. But we'll have time to work on that, now won't we?"

The rain began to fall again as Eclipse flew back to the castle and tucked the would-be prince into bed.

As morning approached, Eclipse wondered if he'd overdone the sleeping spell he'd cast on the boy. As Eclipse sat bedside, he realized that this was probably the first in a long time that the kid had slept in comfort and safety. Eclipse had left the thick, dark curtains over the window closed, choosing to watch the boy in his dragon vision. Even though he expected Sapere Palion to show up, no one knocked at the door. It seemed as if the whole castle slept.

When the boy finally began to rouse, Eclipse got up and went to the door to look out into the hallway. A bucket, towel, and bar of soap sat in the doorway. Eclipse chuckled. The scent had kept everyone away. If only Eclipse had known that was the secret all along...

Maybe the boy would teach Eclipse a thing or two.

Eclipse brought the items inside and set them down beside the bed. Then he went and drew open the curtain to let the sunlight into the room. Last night's storm had left no trace of clouds in the sky, but the ground remained wet.

The boy sat up and stretched. "Where am I?" he asked.

"Three guesses, but only your first one counts," said Eclipse.

"You brought me to the castle to roast me and eat me here." He pushed the blankets off his legs and started to get out of bed. Eclipse saw black streaks all over the sheets from where mud and street filth had rubbed off the boy during the night. One bucket of water was not going to clean him up. He needed a full bath or two.

"As I said," Eclipse continued, "only your first one counts. I intend neither to roast you nor to eat you."

The kid slid out of the bed and glanced down at the bucket on the floor. Again, the boy's stealthy grace caught Eclipse's notice. "What's this?" the kid asked.

"The beginnings of getting you cleaned up."

"Why? If you're not going to eat me but you want me clean, are you going to sacrifice me to your gods? Does some spell require my blood? I won't give it willingly. Look, I might not have a great life, but that doesn't mean that I'm just going to let you take it from me. My soul is all I have and I'm not going to give it to you willingly."

Like an arrow, he got straight to the point. Swiftly, sharply.

Eclipse leaned against the wall and folded his arms over his chest. "Your name is now Calzel. For the time, until your manners become such that you can take the throne, you will be named Prince Calzel of Pillath. You are the future king."

Now it was Calzel's moment to stumble backwards. "Prince?" He wrapped his thin arms around himself. "You're joking me, right?"

Eclipsed pushed away from the wall and knelt down on one knee, lowing his head respectfully. "Prince Calzel, I am your most humble novihomidrak servant, Eclipse." He held out his hands to his sides. "Vochey, Embrace and Opportunity." A gauntlet with short, thick spikes covered his right hand while a scimitar came to his left hand. Eclipse put the scimitar down on the floor before him, then removed the gauntlet and set it near the curved sword. "I set my weapons before you and pledge my oath to serve and protect you as long as you are Prince of Pillath. I will do so again publicly when you are King of Pillath."

"I don't know nothing about being a prince," Calzel protested. "Or how to live like this. I don't even like novihomidraks and I don't want one hunting me down. I appreciate you letting me sleep here and all, but I just want to go back down to my doorway. I need the streets." Calzel looked around, his eyes widening as he looked at the ceiling with an edge of panic. Eclipse watched Calzel visibly shrink back as if a roof over his head was the worst thing he could possibly imagine. "Really, let me outta here."

Calzel ran toward the window. He ran smack into the glass.

"What magic is this?" Calzel asked as he rubbed his nose.

"That's no magic," Eclipse responded. He sent his weapons away for the moment, then rose and went to the window. "It's called glass."

Calzel reached out tentatively and touched the clear surface. "How do you know that it's there?" he asked.

"They are on all the windows of the castle." Eclipse realized this might be new to the boy as he only knew the shuttered windows of the buildings in the city.

"It's cold," Calzel said.

"Yes, but it keeps out the weather and the evils that lurk in the dark better than thin slabs of wood."

"How do we get out of this room then?"

"Through the door."

Calzel shook his head and stepped back as if the doorway wasn't already far enough away from him. "I can't go through there."

"What do you mean?"

"I only sleep in doorways. I can't go through them."

"Why not?" Eclipse asked.

"The archways exist between worlds." As Calzel explained, he began gesturing with his hands to indicate different positions. "If we are here, but we go through a doorway, then we are there, somewhere else."

"I don't understand."

"Last night, we were outside. It was raining. But now we are here. You've transported me through a doorway and now I'm in a different world. A world where you think I'm a prince. I just want to go back to my world."

"How often have you been indoors?"

Calzel looked truly terrified. "In a door? No!"

"Not inside a door," Eclipse laughed. "Inside a building?" He raised his hands to indicate the room they were in.

"You mean, how often have I been transported to another world? Many times. More than I can count."

"You aren't transported to another world," Eclipse

tried to reassure him. "You are just going from one room to another or from outside a building to inside of it."

"No," Calzel shrieked. "That's not what happens."

"Come with me." Eclipse held out his hand toward Calzel. "I'll show you."

Calzel placed his trembling fingers into Eclipse's palm and Eclipse led him to the doorway. Eclipse swung the door open. "Look, it's a hallway." Eclipse stepped through.

Calzel snatched his hand back.

Eclipse walked further down the hallway and turned back toward the boy. "See, I'm still in the same place as you. You can still see me. There's a roof. The floor is the same stone. It's not mystical or magical. Just a doorway."

Calzel retreated as he shook his head.

"Come on through," Eclipse urged.

Calzel refused.

Eclipse went back inside the prince's chambers. "I promise it's okay. Come with me."

Once again, Calzel trusted Eclipse enough to take the novihomidrak's hand. Eclipse walked for the door, feeling Calzel right behind him.

"One easy step and then we're in the hall—"

Calzel was no longer behind him. As the soon-to-be-prince had stepped through the archway of the door, he vanished.

Stunned, Eclipse walked back through the door into the prince's chambers. "Calzel?"

The hairs at the base of Eclipse's neck raised as chills went down his back. Magic pressed through the air and rushed around Eclipse. He turned, slipping into a partial crouch, and he hissed. Through the dragonlids, he swept his gaze around to see if he had missed something. There was nothing, not a trace that Calzel had been there.

As Eclipse straightened, he looked for information on the Humline; what would it have to tell him?

Nothing, though it did seem to smirk. Eclipse felt too old to put up with the antics of the Onesong. Though he aged slowly, he did age, unlike the great energy that ran through the universe and ever renewed itself.

What had the boy said? That if he went through a doorway, he got transported to another world. He had seemed quite sure that it wasn't another room. Had Calzel said anything else? No, but he had tried to go through the window. Windows were safe for him to travel through. The glass had scared him.

Eclipse heard someone round the corner into the hallway. He looked up to see Sapere Palion approaching. Eclipse exited the room, intercepting Palion before the sapere reached the room.

"You have found our Prince?" Palion asked. "What is that stench? Is it coming from the boy, or are you performing more calculations?"

Eclipse didn't want to say that he'd found, then lost the prince. "We're very close, Sapere. It would seem that the boy has left me with a mystery."

"A mystery?"

Eclipse turned Palion around and gave him a light push to start him walking the direction he'd come down the hall. "I need the Wells opened."

"You mean the Prince must come from another world?" the sapere asked. "Is that why the signs were unclear?"

"I'm saying our Prince has a streak of wildness in him."

"Wildness?" Palion asked, glancing back over his shoulder. "Are you saying that he has wild magic?"

"I don't know what it is," Eclipse answered. "But I need to go get him, so I need the Wells opened."

That seemed to press Palion into action. Instead of Eclipse having to push him down the hall, the sapere began to hurry along ahead of Eclipse.

The castle of Pillath had been built around the convergence which opened up this world to the Wells. The first novihomidrak to arrive had been applauded by the world's reigning king of the time. A statue commemorating the king's friendship with that first novihomidrak stood in the hall that led to the door of the room where the convergence was the strongest. On each side of the door stood tall pillars. Eclipse knelt down on a pillow set before the door and rested on his heels while Palion roused two more saperes from their offices.

Eclipse closed his eyes, trying to tune into the Onesong of the universe and the Humline that ran through the fabric of this world. As soon as he felt the faint zing vibrating through him, Eclipse asked his questions of it, "Star 5402 led me to the boy. Where has Calzel gone? Is he still in this universe or has he stepped to another dimension?" As the last inquiry floated through his mind, he knew that was exactly what had happened to Calzel.

He rocked back, hopping up on his feet. "Never mind the Wells," he shouted. "I need a Drifter."

Sapere Palion stopped, his mouth agape, while the other saperes tried their hardest to keep their gazes lowered as they stood behind Palion. "A—ah—a Drifter?"

"You heard me," Eclipse raged, mostly angry at himself for not having seen it sooner. "Our Prince is a Watcher of Worlds who doesn't know who or what he is."

"A Watcher of Worlds is going to be our King?" one of the saperes broke his silence.

Eclipse laughed, finding a supreme humor in their fear. Those who served dragons would cower in terror of a Watcher? "A broken Watcher at that," Eclipse added just to increase their discomfort. "Possibly a wild maege." That ought to make their heads explode.

The saperes who called Pillath their birthplace looked horrified at the thought.

"Someone not born on Pillath cannot be our King," the other sapere protested.

Eclipse rounded on the sapere. "If the Onesong wants you to have a King from a world other than Pillath, then that will be done." He waited to see if the sapere would put up another protest. None came. Still, he caught Palion giving the sapere a don't-push-the-novihomidrak-you-idiot look, and it made Eclipse want to laugh again. He held this chuckle back. "Why are we all standing around? Where's my Drifter? Your soon-to-be-King could be in mortal peril."

The saperes huddled, quickly discussing who the best would be. Then one of the saperes ran off while Palion and the other turned back to Eclipse.

"It may take a moment," Palion said, a tremble in his tone. He shrugged as one corner of his mouth tried to give a smile that he didn't feel fully committed to.

"The maege can be a little tricky to find, as is his nature."

Eclipse turned on his heels. "I will be in my study. Send him directly there when he is ready."

Eclipse heard Palion sigh after he muttered some confirming acknowledgement. If only Eclipse could show them what a novihomidrak was truly capable of. He stormed off down the hallway, his black cloak sweeping noisily over the stone floor.

Back in his study, he sat at his desk and stared out the window. At least yesterday with the storm, he'd had some entertainment to go along with his irritation. Today, the livestock boys were going through their normal routine of walking the pigs and feeding the chickens while Eclipse could do nothing but wait. He wondered if there were any calculations he could make in helping the Drifter to find the boy. If he could narrow down the number of chaos doors they had to walk through…

It doesn't work like that and you know it, a little voice in Eclipse's head nagged.

There's got to be some way to trace the boy, Eclipse countered. He couldn't just sit here and do nothing.

Grabbing some parchment and his quill, he set to working out preliminary calculations. Once he'd emptied his mind of the early thoughts that came to him and he'd scratched out several false starts, he recopied all the correct calculations out onto a new paper. Then he went to the bookshelf where he pulled the usual book from the shelf. No dust would settle on the wood again today.

Setting the book on the calculations, he put his hands on the book and said, "Novestri ali'ack suventay," while looking at it through his dragonlids. When he removed his hands, the book flipped open of its own accord. The pages were blank.

Eclipse growled into his hands as he rubbed his face. Why was he being mocked?

"Be bRAVE," came the ink to the surface of the page.

Chills swept down his arms, but as he went to slam the book closed, he realized he wasn't alone. Was the rising gooseflesh an alert to someone's presence or to the cryptic message of the book? Either way, Eclipse stood as he turned to face the newcomer.

At the doorway, a very frightened sapere stood near an old man in a worn gray cloak. His dark, intense eyes spoke of things he'd seen without needing to say a word and told Eclipse that he was a Drifter. Leaning heavily on a walking stick, the man had a hold of the sapere by the collar of the sapere's black robes. The Drifter released the sapere, dropping the sapere to his feet, as the Drifter spoke in a rough tone. "I hear you are in need of my services."

"I am," Eclipse said with a firm step forward. "I need to walk between dimensions."

The Drifter raised a thick eyebrow. "Tricky business... taking novihomidraks through chaos doors."

Eclipse inhaled, making sure that he stood just a couple inches taller, and rolled his shoulders back. "You will be well compensated for any dangers you face with a bonus for my safe return. The saperes will see to your payment. You may request a deposit if you like."

The sapere's eyes widened in alarm and he looked like he wanted to raise a protest, but upon remembering who he was with in the room, he clamped his mouth shut tight.

The Drifter nodded. "Which dimension are we traveling to?" He folded both hands over the round top knob of the walking stick and leaned into it.

"I don't know," Eclipse answered. "I'll need you to do a trace."

Grunting, the Drifted tipped his head a little to the side and his mouth pulled momentarily into a sneer. "Tracking is extra."

"Whatever you need. Any components that you use will be compensated or resupplied."

The Drifter's brown-eyed gaze swept around the room. "Must be pretty special, this person you're looking for."

"Enough so that we're willing to make sure you are well cared for in a way that maintains our privacy as well."

The sapere's face reddened. Eclipse swore that he could see steam coming right off of him.

The Drifter's eyes narrowed, as he if suspected something. "Is this coming from the council?"

"No," Eclipse countered quickly. "The Dragon Council is unaware of the situation at present and, I hope, will remain that way."

"Good luck with that," the sapere muttered under his breath, "the way you are spending money."

Eclipse knew the Drifter's ears wouldn't pick up the sapere's words, but Eclipse's heightened novihomidrak senses did. He suspected that was the sapere's intent, though it would certainly call for a report to Palion to give a reprimand for the sapere's behavior and remind them all of what could happen to a tattletale.

The Drifter began to nod beneath the hood of his dark gray cloak. He reached up to lower it, revealing long silver hair beneath, as he reached out to shake Eclipse's hand. "Looks like you've hired yourself a trip through chaos."

Eclipse let the Drifter follow the sapere out to find Palion and arrange for payment to be made while Eclipse headed to his quarters to dress for the trip. He chose brown pants which were moderately tight but had lots of pockets and loops. Around this, he put on his weapons belt which held a couple non-magical daggers. Then he added a white, short sleeve tunic which laced up behind his neck and left most of his back bare. Calling his weapons to hand, he slid the sword in its scabbard and clipped the gauntlet to a loop. He topped the whole thing with a sparkling black cape which he'd had specially made for him shortly after taking the position here on Pillath. He didn't often have occasion to wear it.

Eclipse scoffed. He didn't have the opportunity to use his skills as a novihomidrak frequently either.

Which meant it felt extra nice to have the sacred cloak wrapped around his shoulders again. The top section was a hooded caplet which hung down as far as his shoulder blades and covered where his tunic didn't. The main part of the cloak hung off his shoulders, leaving the open back hidden beneath the caplet. It clasped together in front with a hook and chain across his chest and allowed him to reach beneath and easily get to his weapons. The whole thing was designed so that he could extend his wings and take flight into a night sky, a shimmering mirage against the stars.

Viewing himself in the mirror now, Eclipse let the

dragon wings surface, extend, and stretch. He rolled his shoulders, a proud feeling glowing through his chest. He loved being a novihomidrak. He blinked, letting the dragonlids stay down, his golden aura now visible as it surrounded him and his wings. He tossed his long black hair, shaking it gently for a moment before pulling it back into a thick band and securing the ends. Long hair was one thing, letting it become an obstacle during a fight was another.

Did he feel a fight coming on?

Eclipse closed his eyes, letting the Onesong fill his mind. He went beyond the Humline of this world, seeking the central energy which flowed through all things.

Yes, there was a fight coming. But not what he would expect. This battle would be different.

Whatever it would be, he would enjoy it. It had been a long time since he'd been allowed to be his novihomidrak self. Now, he would be off-world, in another dimension even, facing chaos at the core. He had been born for this. Literally!

Retracting the wings and tucking away every other aspect of him that showed his dragon side, Eclipse left the room and headed for Sapere Palion's office. A loud argument behind the closed door erupted as Eclipse drew close. Quickening his steps, Eclipse entered the room without knocking.

The Drifter was currently halfway across the room as if he were storming out while the saperes stood behind Palion's desk, all three of them leaning forward on their arms over the desk. Their mouths all snapped shut as Eclipse entered. The Drifter, meanwhile, had a hiccup in his limping step which caused a momentary pause before he started forward again.

"Is there a problem?" Eclipse asked.

The Drifter rolled his eyes. "I require an eighty percent deposit for this mission. Chaos doors do not come cheaply for novihomidraks. I have expenses and I need to make payment ahead of time to certain... parties... to insure your safe travel. They refuse to let me leave with my money. They think I'll just take off with it and never return. I just want to make sure that I have a good share collecting interest while I'm away."

Eclipse shook his head as he crossed to the sapere's desk. "For the love of the Onesong!" He snatched the banded stack of bills from beneath Palion's hand and returned it to the Drifter. As he handed it over, he said over his shoulders to the saperes, "He is our ally, not our enemy."

A surprised softness entered the Drifter's eyes. "Thank you," he muttered. "Don't often meet someone that feels that way."

"I want to return safely just as much as you do," Eclipse remarked. "Go make your arrangements and your deposits."

The Drifter stepped to the side and vanished with his handful of money.

"I will go right to the Dragon Council if he doesn't return," Palion shouted.

"It's the kingdom's money, not theirs. Do you really think they are likely to care?" Eclipse walked over to the desk and stared Palion in the eyes. "Now, if you would prefer Pillath to go on without a king and wars to erupt between the towns that cannot control their ambitions, then by all means keep defying me."

Palion dropped down into his chair but continued to glare up at Eclipse as he wrapped his fingers tightly around the carved wooden armrests. "And if you still cannot find the would-be king?"

These words, more than anything else Palion had said or done today, angered Eclipse. "You would accuse a novihomidrak of failure?"

The other saperes took a step back and lowered their gazes, but Palion would not be cowed. He leaned forward on the desk. "I am almost beginning to think that you are stalling. Would there be a reason that you would have a war? Needing to save the world, are you?"

"Ah," said Eclipse, "you do accuse this novihomidrak of needing unrest and misery to fulfill my natural instincts." He leaned in closer to Palion and smiled, the dragon teeth coming down as he did so. He knew it would misshape his face slightly and, for a moment, fill his mouth with the taste of blood, but it would be worth it to remind Palion who he was dealing with. "You would do well, Sapere, to remember your place. You are my servant."

The Drifter reappeared.

Eclipse turned with a snarl.

"If now's a bad time…" the Drifter began.

Eclipse glared back at Palion to make sure the sapere cowered respectfully, before shaking off the dragon aspect. "No. Your timing is nearly perfect."

"Good. Arrangements are being made," the Drifter replied gruffly. He raised his walking stick, held it out to the right, then released it. The walking stick vanished. "Show me where I need to start tracking."

Eclipse led the way, but as he left the room, he threw one last irritated look back at the saperes. Leading the

Drifter up the stairs, Eclipse went to the chambers where he'd last seen Calzel, but he did not enter the room. He knew how important precise details were. From the hallway, he indicated the door. "It was here, in the doorway as he crossed the threshold."

The Drifter held up his hands and inched closer to the door. "Going in or coming out?"

"We were coming out."

Reaching toward the top of the doorframe, the Drifter wiggled his fingers as he slowly extended his arms toward the center. There was a snap and the Drifter jumped back. He looked at his finger for a moment, then stuck it in his mouth to suck on it. "You've got yourself a powerful curse there," the Drifter said around his finger.

"A curse?" Eclipse let the plain fact sink in.

The Drifter took his finger from his mouth and wiped the appendage on his tattered gray robe to dry it. "How did you get this person into the castle? You couldn't have walked him through the doors."

"I did."

"How? There must be more."

"I had cast a sleep spell on him."

The Drifter's eyes widened with enlightenment. "Ah! Novihomidrak magic overshadows this curse. That is good news for you."

"If I want to tie my magic to him so he can walk through doors!"

Shrugging, the Drifter said, "We all have to make sacrifices for others somewhere."

"He told me he cannot walk through any doorway and each time he does, he ends up in another world." After standing in the hallway for so long, Eclipse wondered why he'd never realized that this royal chamber was so much darker than the others. Maybe the curse on the boy brought a darkness with it. Or maybe, Eclipse pondered, the Drifter came with his own shadows. "He wanted to climb out the window."

The Drifter continued to inspect the doorway along with the dark wood and stone which surrounded it. "Windows, good. Doors, bad. Got it. I wonder how long it took him to figure this out?"

Eclipse really didn't care about that detail. "Can you find him or not?"

"Would help if I knew who had cursed him and why? What do you know about him?"

"He's a boy, around twelve years of age. Abandoned. Smells terrible."

The Drifter lowered his hands and turned to face Eclipse. "You didn't bring him to the castle because you pitied him. It still stinks in here, by the way. Why bring a smelly boy here?"

Eclipse didn't want to answer that.

"He is the next king, isn't he? The whole kingdom knows there were no heirs, but certainly our prophet of Pillath would be searching for the new ruler."

Eclipse felt his gaze drop to the floor and he knew that one action was enough for the Drifter to know his answer.

The Drifter began to snicker. "So, the next king is a cursed Drifter."

"Watcher of Worlds, actually," Eclipse said, glad that he could finally get in a piece of information that would shock the Drifter and felt pleased when the Drifter's eyes widened to nearly double in size at the news.

"You're sure about that?" the Drifter asked, the shock evident in his voice.

"I am. The signs I kept getting in my search for the prince were unclear. His magic is wild and that was something I hadn't accounted for."

"So how does that point to him being a Watcher? That's quite a leap in your guess."

"I found him in a doorway. He said he'd been watching me for a while, but for all the times I'd gone down that alleyway seeking him, I'd never sensed him."

"Ah," the Drifter growled in confirmation, "sounds like a Watcher." He stepped inside the room and started examining the doorway from the prince's chambers.

"We are going to be able to get him, right?"

"Chaos doors may seem like illogical combination locks, but when you've walked through as many as I have, they start to make sense."

Eclipse wasn't sure he understood exactly what the Drifter was getting at, but he kept his mouth closed while the thought of going through that many chaos doors made him shiver. It looked bad for a noviho-midrak to seem like he didn't know everything or to appear scared.

"Ah, his magic is wild," the Drifter confirmed. He waved Eclipse into the room, then pointed at a spot on the stone.

Eclipse moved in close to see what the Drifter was pointing at, but the smell nearly made Eclipse back away. He flinched at the sulfuric odor emanating from the dark pinhole. He swore a light whiff of smoke curled out from it.

"That's where his magic retaliated against the curse. Or tried to." The Drifter straightened and took a glance around the room. "I would bet that every doorway he's walked through would have one of these, probably in the same spot."

The stench that came off the boy might have been his own magic oozing around him like a protective shield. Had that remnant in the stone been how Eclipse had known that the boy had wild magic? That the smell been a warning?

"Get something that was the boy's."

Eclipse looked around the room for something the boy had dropped. Having only the clothes on his back, there was nothing that Calzel had left behind. But the bed hadn't been made, so Eclipse checked the pillow for one of the boy's hairs. He did manage to find one.

"A hair? Really?" the Drifter gruffly asked, his lips in a sneer. "Do you know how much that thing reeks?"

"It's all I've got of the boy's. He didn't have much to begin with."

"Well, find a way to keep it with you. Preferably some way that traps the smell away. We'll be needing that hair later."

"Vochey case." A little clasping box, slightly larger than a locket appeared in Eclipse's hand from his room. He dropped the hair onto the red velvet lining of the box, latched the lid closed, and stuck it in his pouch.

Meanwhile, the Drifter had stepped into the doorway and looked up at the stone. He reached up and rubbed at it. "Yeah, I'll be able to follow him," the Drifter confirmed. "Can't promise you he'll still be in the same spot. Depends on how frightened he was when he arrived."

"I think he's use to it."

"Doesn't mean the Shift was pleasant for him. Especially if his magic is trying to stop this sort of thing from happening." The Drifter lowered his hands, putting one of them on his hip. "You ever experienced chaos lightning?"

Eclipse didn't like the sound of it. Ordinary lightning wouldn't hurt him, but anything preceded by the word chaos was never a good thing, especially for a novi-homidrak. "Is that a possibility here?"

When the Drifter smiled, Eclipse knew he had good reason to fear. Even more, he knew why the Onesong had ordered him to be brave. "Ah, we'll have a storm all right. Ready?" the Drifter asked.

Eclipse nodded. The sooner he got this over with, the sooner he could return with the prince.

The Drifter landed a heavy hand on Eclipse's shoulder. "Step to the right," the Drifter ordered.

Just to make sure that Eclipse did what he was instructed, the Drifter pulled on Eclipse.

The hairs at the base of Eclipse's neck raised like hackles. Shocks of lightning sprang over his skin. Every dragon aspect took over Eclipse as rage filled him.

"Easy now," the Drifter said. "It's over."

Eclipse looked around, huffing as he searched for any danger around him. He curled his fingers, feeling the dragon claws pressing into his palms.

"Really," the Drifter said, "we're through. There's no danger."

Eclipse whirled completely around. "Chaos," he growled in a voice even deeper than the Drifter's.

"No, no chaos followed us."

The Drifter's words didn't completely reassure Eclipse. Only the hazy memory of their mission brought him some calm. "The boy... is he on this dimension?"

"I don't see any structures around. If you don't either, then he may have actually rebounded out of this world to another. A sophisticated curse would ping him through multiple worlds just to make sure he was so lost that he'd never find his way back."

Eclipse shivered as he contemplated going through wave after wave of chaos as magic spun him around until he was completely lost. "Who would do such a thing to a child?"

"Chances are, it was done to him to spite his parents."

Eclipse still wondered what kind of person could plan and enact such a curse upon a child. Unfortunately, he knew the answer all too well. The connections he'd had with the multitude of Humlines on different worlds over his span as a novihomidrak had taught him many things about the varied minds of people and their self-regarding intents. Humanity had always been painfully savage upon each other and the other races they dominated.

Finding a focus for his anger in the Drifter's statement, Eclipse looked around. The forest trees twisted around, growing in dense curls in a fight to survive. He and the Drifter were on a path. Eclipse went to the top of the rise and looked around with his dragon vision. He saw nothing but tangled forest branches.

"He's not here?" Eclipse said. He turned to find the Drifter looking at trees near where they had landed.

"Ah, here!" The Drifter pointed to a branch.

Eclipse saw from where he was that the Drifter was indicating a pinpoint hole in the wood. It still emanated sparks, which didn't seem to matter to the Drifter as the man began exploring around it with his fingers. Now Eclipse could feel the pull of the Onesong working through the Drifter, and Eclipse briefly wondered why he hadn't noticed it before.

Eclipse felt a pull through his gut as the Drifter encountered the next chaos door and Eclipse rocked on his feet, his vision swirling.

The Drifter looked back at him. "You all right? Wanna sit this one out?"

As if that was even a possibility! "No," Eclipse said, blinking his eyes to refocus. "Where ever the prince is, he's bound to be scared. He will at least recognize me."

"That doesn't mean he'll be none too happy to see you. Hope you have a plan for catching him if he tries to go diving through another door." The Drifter walked over to Eclipse and, without warning, clasped a hand behind his neck and pushed him sideways through the dimensions.

It was one of Eclipse's extended wings which pushed the Drifter away from him as they dawned into the new realm.

"Warning next time," Eclipse growled. He knew that even as threating as he sounded, the Drifter still probably wouldn't give him notice.

"Another realm he would bounce out of," the Drifter announced.

As the Drifter began to search for the pinpoint hole they knew would be nearby, Eclipse listened to the Humline. "Something approaches," Eclipse warned, even as he extended his senses along the Humline of this world to discover what danger rushed toward them. His first impression was that it was a dragon.

He saw the speck on the horizon through his dragon vision. The on comer knew what Eclipse was; the

Humline had warned of his intrusion. The black dot in the sky vanished. Eclipse felt it drawing closer.

"Hurry," Eclipse said, nudging the Drifter.

"I have to assure the next door is clear.

"Do it now. We have another novihomidrak coming. He's going to try to stop us."

The Drifter paused and in that lifetime span of only a few seconds, Eclipse felt the hesitation ripple through the fabric of the world.

The novihomidrak appeared, swinging his crude iron sword wide. Eclipse had no time to put on his gauntlet or draw his weapon.

"Found it," the Drifter shouted.

Eclipse stood with a magical shield extended between him and the other novihomidrak. Blond hair hung in tangles around the man's face, knotting into a matted long beard. The dragonlids were green.

"We mean you no harm," Eclipse shouted.

The novihomidrak only grunted and pressed harder on the shield.

The Drifter seized Eclipse's robes and yanked him hard. "Hold on," Eclipse heard the Drifter shout before they slid between dimensions.

Eclipse felt himself shaking. Blue sparks surrounded him in the same way cinders pop in the air after a log is tossed onto a fire and struck him with surprising force. As his dragon aspects once again took him over, through his dragon vision, the shift in dimensions went from blackness all around him to a tunnel streaked with white and gray as they sped along its length. Fireworks exploded along the walls, extending out with jagged lines of lightning.

An iron blade struck Eclipse's arm, tearing a ragged cut through the material covering him.

The Drifter grunted as they seemingly struck a wall and came to a dead stop. Both Eclipse and the Drifter dropped to the floor of the tunnel. The streaking lines settled like fog around them. Eclipse rose up, trying to get above the mist to look around but the clouds were all around them.

"Get down," the Drifter yelled, tugging on Eclipse's robes.

"The novihomidrak followed us." He slid his hand into his spiked gauntlet and freed it from the loop.

"It's the chaos, you fool. We've got to get moving again."

Sharp toothed lines rolled up Eclipse's legs. "Chaos," Eclipse hissed, beginning to tear at the tendrils, which snapped around his fingers and fully ensnared him.

"Yes, chaos! Now let's go."

The Drifter pushed Eclipse once more and they finished speeding through the tunnel, emerging into a world so bright that Eclipse had to shield his eyes against the glare. He hesitated only a moment, knowing that he might still be in danger. Venturing a peek, Eclipse saw the uneven lines were gone from around him. "It's bright here," Eclipse muttered, figuring that the Drifter wouldn't even care about it.

As predicted, the Drifter shrugged and started looking around. "Well, at least this place is more promising. It wouldn't be an effective curse if he landed on a planet without doors."

"Why set the curse to take effect on doorways?"

"Watchers of Worlds see things through doorways and similar spaces. They specifically look for people and events. When they want to, they can reach through and grab objects. You said you found him sleeping in a doorway, but you never figured out why he liked doorways."

"No." That was part of the puzzle Eclipse still didn't understand. If Calzel was so afraid of doorways, why did he sleep in them? Calzel had even said that he'd been watching Eclipse for several nights, yet Eclipse had never noticed the boy there.

The Drifter sent Eclipse a hard, level gaze. "When he's got a relaxed focus, he can probably get his magic attuned enough to slide into a world that he wishes to go. Much like how your novihomidrak magic overcame the curse, he probably figured out that his own magic, when channeled properly, can do the same thing. It's got to be a very, very precise state that he has to be in and one he's practiced. Otherwise, the curse would bounce him around."

"So you're saying he wanted to be in Pillath?" Eclipse tried to look at the Drifter to see if there was anything more in the man's body language that would tell Eclipse what the Drifter was really thinking and saying, but the sun's glare forced him to keep his head down and his eyes still shaded.

"Or he knew that you could help him."

Eclipse knocked a stone with his foot, sending it rolling further in the street. All he had done for the boy was to force him to go through a doorway and reactivate the curse. The boy could have done that on his own, without Eclipse's *help*. "I'm not sure I've done that much."

"I shall keep my hopes that this is all part of destiny. We should be moving along."

Finally adjusting to the light, Eclipse dared to lower

his hand away from his eyes. He blinked and looked around to see several tall buildings around them.

"You all right?" the Drifter asked and nodded toward his arm.

In the skirmish with chaos, Eclipse had forgotten the injury. The novihomidrak's blade had cut him. More irritating, the sword had cut his cloak. Eclipse looked through the hole in the fabric and saw that the injury wasn't deep. The barbarian novihomidrak's weapon hadn't been very sharp. The cut would heal in time. "I'm fine," Eclipse reported.

"I certainly hope so. My price goes up if you start leaving a blood trail through the dimensions."

"That won't be happening." Eclipse ran his hand over his arm and cast a light spell to heal the wound. It would take a sapere to fully heal it for him and now it might even need to be cut back open, but finding Calzel took priority over a simple injury like this. The full needs of his healing could be seen to later, along with the laughter the saperes would get over Eclipse letting himself get hurt so senselessly. He should have been paying more attention. He was lucky the Drifter had stayed with him as they went through the chaos door. If Eclipse had stopped, but the Drifter hadn't, Eclipse might not even be standing here with him. Would the barbarian novihomidrak have been able to come into the chaos door? He shivered at the thought.

"Nice costume," a stranger said, walking by them. "Wrong time of year."

It woke Eclipse's awareness to the fact that the street they were on was filled with traffic and people.

"Snap out of it. I need your head in the game here," the Drifter said. He stepped away from Eclipse muttering as he went, "The vibrations of this world are close to Pillath's. Guess the curse wouldn't be any good if there was no one around to frighten the boy or pull him through doorways against his will."

Eclipse knew the last remark was made to slight him.

"I wonder how many Ghost Worlds he's seen. Those are scary even when you know what's happening," the Drifter said and Eclipse thought he saw a shiver go through the man's shoulders at the thought.

Eclipse tucked his wings away, but looked around with his dragon vision. There were no special auras nearby, no trails or tracks, nothing that stuck out of the ordinary. Buildings towered overhead higher than any of the castle turrets. Several engine vehicles zipped by in the streets. What this world did seem to have was an overabundance of doors. If Calzel decided to run, it wouldn't be hard for him to make an escape.

"No holes," the Drifter announced after inspecting the nearby doorways. "I'll need the item you brought for him to see if his vibration is on this world."

Eclipse pulled out the case and handed the hair toward the Drifter, who looked at it with disgust. "Damn thing still stinks," complained the Drifter as he held out his hand while wrinkling up his nose.

"Then you'll be twice as revolted when we discover the boy," Eclipse said.

The Drifter gave a disgusted growl but let Eclipse drop the hair onto his palm. After a moment, the hair lifted into the air. "Well, he's here. All we need now is a stuffed up bloodhound to track him." The hair settled back down on the Drifter's palm and he indicated for Eclipse to take it back.

Eclipse put it once again in the box and returned it to his pouch.

"I've tracked him this far," the Drifter added. "Now it's up to you."

"You make it sound so easy."

The Drifter gave a carefree shrug and a non-committal grunt. Unfortunately, he wasn't wrong. His job, for the moment, was done and it now rested on Eclipse's shoulders to find and secure the boy.

Eclipse closed his eyes and listened. At first, all he heard was the sounds of the city around him: people chatting, sirens whining, music playing. He allowed himself to deepen into the resonances, relaxing until the noise fell away and he began to hear the zing he sought to tune into.

Even though he'd spent the night watching the boy sleep, Eclipse didn't really have a good image of the boy to hold in his mind. He did, however, have the emotions of what it felt like to carry Calzel back to the castle as well as the efforts of looking for him. Star 5402. That guide point wouldn't even exist here in a different world of a dimensional universe.

So what did he need to look for here?

The Humline of this world zipped an answer back to him. He couldn't say that it made sense though. Five thousand four hundred and two stars.

"What do you know about this world?" Eclipse asked. "I need somewhere with a lot of stars."

The Drifter gave a look around, his thick, shaggy eyebrows raising on his forehead with the direction that he looked in. "Can't say I've ever been here before. Can't say I haven't been either. My line of work takes me a lot of places. You're an old novihomidrak. Do you remember every world you've saved?"

"Fair point," Eclipse answered. He knew that as a novihomidrak, he looked to be a human in his late thirties, maybe early forties. But much like dragons, he just aged slowly now. His real age was many times that and, much like a dragon, he'd lost count of his true age. Bouncing between worlds with all their different orbital cycles and calendars did that to a person. Still, it would be nice if the Drifter could help him out a little more. Like attracts like, after all.

With that realization, Eclipse went over to the Drifter and pulled a gray hair off the man's head.

"Ow!" the Drifter protested, putting a hand to his head. For a moment, Eclipse thought the Drifter might punch him, but the old man just glared.

"Maybe next time you'd like a warning," Eclipse said in a snarky tone as he felt the little shine of revenge in his chest.

"You novihomidraks are bastards, each and every one of you." As he said the words, a tiny grin came to his lips. "Maybe next time through, I'll drop you in the middle of chaos."

Even though he doubted the Drifter would actually do that, it still gave Eclipse a shiver. Unfortunately, the Drifter knew he had the upper hand on it too. Rather than bothering with trying to deny the threat or make a hasty ill-suited apology, Eclipse took Calzel's hair back out of the box and loosely knotted it together with the strand he'd taken from the Drifter. Allowing himself a deep breath, Eclipse let dragon magic rumble through him. "Sho'dan exsa caulrae." The magic burst from him, making his head whirl a bit. As the momentary light-headedness faded, a bubble formed in front of Eclipse.

The Drifter moved closer.

The image of Calzel walking down a cobblestone street swirled inside the shimmery surface of the bubble. The boy gazed around, as if the sights scared him. He even glanced back over his shoulder a couple of times as if he were looking to see if he was being followed. Eclipse knew that he couldn't see another around Calzel because the spell only allowed him to see Calzel's energy and not anyone else's. For all Eclipse knew, the boy was about to be stabbed in the back and Eclipse had no way to warn him.

Eclipse moved his hand along the outside of the bubble, careful not to touch it. The picture inside changed to show more of what was around the boy. The buildings were stone and driverless wagons went through the streets. None of the surroundings looked like this world.

"Ah, clever, clever little curse," the Drifter muttered. "It brought him to this world, just not to this time."

They watched as Calzel crouched close to a doorway and waved his hand over the opening. He was careful not to cross the threshold. Eclipse tried to refocus the image of the bubble to see what Calzel was looking at, but the boy's body remained in the way and Eclipse couldn't find a good angle. Then Calzel started flipping the pictures that he saw as if he were reading a book.

"What do you think he's looking for?" Eclipse asked.

"If I was a cursed Watcher of Worlds' powers, I'd be looking for home every time I landed on a new world. It might take a few days or weeks to go through every world in this dimension, but the boy has that time as long as he doesn't go through another doorway."

"Can you identify the time period and get us there?"

The Drifter looked at him like Eclipse should know better. "I'm a Drifter, not a Watcher of Worlds."

Small difference, Eclipse thought. Granted, he was sure that the full extent of the Drifter's abilities were probably as much of a mystery to Eclipse as the powers of a novihomidrak were not fully known to a Drifter.

But the Drifter smiled and held up a finger. "Ah, but this is why you hired me, right? You knew I was good. I made arrangements, didn't I?"

Yes, the Drifter had said he had to get things into place, prepayments to be made. Eclipse badly wanted to ask how the Drifter had known that the boy would be found in another time, but maybe it had just been a fortunate guess. Or maybe the Drifter knew more about this curse than he was letting on.

The Drifter saw Eclipse's examination and a smile ticked across the Drifter's lips, but he wasn't forthcoming with an explanation. It seemed as if he intentionally wanted Eclipse to stew in thought. According to the Humline of this world, the Drifter meant no ill-will toward Eclipse, only a little mischief, so Eclipse didn't press it.

Had the Humline indicated through their connection that the Drifter's intent was different, then Eclipse would have felt inclined to be a little more aggressive. As it stood, they both had secrets in their pockets and Eclipse had no desire to show his full hand to the Drifter. He was certain the Drifter felt the same.

Eclipse dismissed the bubble and whispered, "Strakae cazidor." The Drifter's hair burned quickly away from Calzel's. The magic left a charred scent on top of the boy's odor. As the hair drifted toward the ground, uncurling from the knot as it went, Eclipse caught the strand in the box once more.

"I fought pretty hard with the saperes for your funds. It will take several months for me to repair those relationships, and it might include a fight with the council too. Prove you were worth the trouble and the money," Eclipse said.

The Drifter reached his hand out to the right and his walking stick reappeared and glided into his palm. A little slip of paper rolled up in a cylinder and tied with a ribbon hung from his walking stick. The Drifter slid the ribbon away from the paper, unfurled the message, and read it before wadding it up and shoving the mangled paper in his pocket. He tugged the ribbon from his walking stick and let it fall to the ground. "Follow me," the Drifter said as he whipped around and started hobbling down the street.

The weary tension of being in an unknown world pressed into the muscles of Eclipse's back. He shifted his gaze back and forth, constantly aware of his surroundings, as he followed the Drifter through the streets. He noted not only the people looking at them, but the cameras that watched them. Of course, two men in long cloaks probably wasn't something you saw here every day. The presence of magic in this world was also irregular. Eclipse wondered if anyone of this world could even feel the enchantments which naturally surrounded himself and the Drifter. He highly doubted it.

By the time they had rounded the fifth corner and walked down the multitude of blocks, Eclipse snapped, "Where are we going?"

"This isn't an exact science," the Drifter growled back.

Eclipse figured he better let the Drifter have his lead here and followed along in silence, still feeling edgy. Something about this world just seemed to be under his skin and he couldn't figure out why. Had he been here before? He wasn't sure. Something just struck him as familiar and yet alien at the same time. Eclipse searched the Humline to see if there was another novihomidrak. Could that be the reason why he felt such an unsettled ease? A novihomidrak from another clan might make him feel like this. Might. He'd encountered enough of them on other worlds to know that novihomidraks usually had their reasons for being there and they generally left each other alone to do their jobs. It wasn't always the case. Sometimes one novihomidrak needed to hunt another down. Yet he didn't feel that was the circumstances here. But he had already encountered one novihomidrak whose intention had been to stop them. Would there be more? The Humline returned no answer for him. Eclipse had to say that the lack of replies from the Humline sure made it difficult to trust it. Be brave, the Humline of his current world, his current assignment, had told him. What exactly did that mean? What exactly did it know that he would have to face?

They came to a strip mall and the Drifter looked curiously along the short length of it. "I wonder if she doesn't realize that she's a Drifter," he commented as he set his hand on the red bricks.

"She? Who are we looking for?"

"An oracle." The Drifter started walking along the doorways of each business very slowly.

"I thought you said she was a Drifter." Eclipse stood

back, sensing that the Drifter was trying to feel something and Eclipse didn't want own magical aura interfering with what the Drifter was trying to do.

"All Drifters start off as oracles. Not every oracle can advance. But Drifters have to have some sort of sense of the future. It's that same ability which allows us to shift to other worlds in a realm. Very powerful Drifters eventually learn how to go through chaos doors to alternate dimensions." After a momentary pause, the Drifter grimaced as he clenched his fists. "She's close," the Drifter growled, "but something else is shielding her."

"Can you tell who?" Eclipse asked.

"If I had my guess, it would be another Drifter. Maybe someone who doesn't want the boy found."

"As though they knew we were coming?"

"Something like that. But how?" The Drifter looked at the line of shops along the strip mall again. "Or maybe the better question is when did they know that we would be following him?"

"When?" Eclipse inquired.

"This has to be arranged. Someone does not want us to find the boy."

"Can you tell how old the spells is?"

Again, the Drifter's lips twitched and he gave a small chuckle. "You wouldn't believe me, but I'm going to say at least seven hundred years."

Eclipse understood the implications immediately. Someone had known for seven hundred years that Eclipse and the Drifter were going to come looking for the boy. Eclipse had to wonder how long the boy had been traveling under his curse. Maybe the boy's age was a curse too.

The Drifter pointed to a door. "Here. I'll let you open this."

"What's going to happen when I open the door?" Eclipse asked.

"Don't know," the Drifter shrugged. "But if they were smart enough to cast shielding spell, they might've been smart enough to set another curse. I don't want to be cursed forever. I'll let the novihomidrak take that on."

Eclipse stalked over to the door, refusing to show the Drifter any fear, and pulled on the handle while snarling, "Thanks." As the Drifter started to walk through the door, Eclipse added, "Who's to say the curse isn't in the doorway?"

The Drifter was mid-step as Eclipse had said his words and tried to pull back, but instead he just staggered awkwardly on his old hips. The Drifter turned, standing halfway in the doorway and half out of it. "Now that's not a very nice thing to do to a guy."

The more time Eclipse spent with him, the more Eclipse really started to like the Drifter. The older man had a good sense of humor about things.

Pictures of sandy beaches, towering castles, and biking trails through a forest graced the light blue walls of the business. It smelled faintly of cleaning supplies, save for the one spot near the receptionist's desk where she had a candle burning. From the doorway, Eclipse could read the label: Sugar Cookie. It made his mouth water a little bit.

The Drifter walked across the gray carpet passed all the racks of travel brochures to the desk set toward the back of the room where a brunette woman in her late twenties sat behind a flat panel computer monitor. She briefly looked up at the Drifter and eyed him over. "Can

I help you?" she asked, her tone indicating that the only travel she suspected he would be doing was to the local homeless shelter.

"I'm looking for Amanda Bellock," the Drifter replied.

The tension entering her tightened the muscles of her throat and flashed red into her pale blue aura.

"Why? What business do you have with her?" the woman answered, doing a surprisingly good job of keeping trepidation out of her voice.

"I just need to speak to you," the Drifter said, setting an open hand upon her desk and leaning forward slightly. Then, he added in a lower tone, "About your visions."

Now she looked dead out frightened. She pushed her chair back from her desk, her body tilting as if to make a dash for it. Her gaze sprinted between the Drifter and Eclipse. When she realized she had no way out, she settled back and grasped the arm rests of her chair. "I don't do that anymore," she softly protested, her voice full of shame.

The Drifter yanked back a chair from near the wall, dropped it in front of her desk, and plopped down into it. "Well you do now, sister." He crossed his arms over his chest.

For a moment, fear flooded her eyes and Eclipse thought she might rise up in anger. But the anxiety won. "I can't do it," she said meekly. "All my life people have made fun of me and called me a witch. I'm finally getting all that behind me. My life is normal now."

"Normal?" the Drifter growled deeply. "As if."

"Please, leave me alone."

The Drifter broke out in a full out snarl. "I hate people like you that deny their power."

"Fortunately for me, you can't make me use my powers," Amanda said.

The Drifter shrugged and jerked his thumb over his shoulder toward Eclipse. "Do you know what he is? He is a novihomidrak. That means that he's a beast at getting his mission completed. He doesn't care who or what stands in his way. He'll go through them. And there isn't a damn thing you can do about it. For him, you are just another piece in his mission and he is unstoppable and nearly immortal."

With the thread of tension coming off of Amanda, Eclipse felt an electric surge go through him. Amanda had done something. He searched the Humline for that precise movement that indicated what action she had taken. She had pressed a buzzer and set off an alarm. She believed that help was on the way.

A moment later the phone rang and she didn't make a move to answer it. She just let it ring. Eclipse walked over to the phone and picked it up. "Hello?"

Amanda looked at him in horror as Eclipse used her voice to answer the phone.

"We've received an alarm from your location. Is everything okay?" the man on the other end of the line asked.

"Everything is fine here," Eclipse said, still using Amanda's voice. "I accidentally hit the buzzer. It's a false alarm."

Amanda jumped out of her seat and reached for the phone. Eclipse held it beyond her grasp. "It's not a false alarm!" she screamed.

"Just to be sure, can I have your verification code?" the man on the other end asked.

Verification code. Eclipse searched the Humline, again looking for that precise moment in time when she had set the code. No, it wasn't her. Her employer had set the code. Of course. The employer had given his employees the code just in case things like this had happened. Eclipse looked for that moment and found it even while Amanda still stood there screaming that it wasn't a false alarm and that she really was under attack. Eclipse knew her pleas would never be heard. He'd shielded the phone the moment he had picked it up. "The code is 'four evergreen trees.'"

Amanda stopped mid-scream, her mouth now hanging open. She knew that there was no way that he could have known that, as if speaking in her voice was something that anyone could do naturally. She dropped back down into her chair, the stunned expression never leaving her face.

"Good," the man said. "I've confirmed false alarm. You're good to go. Have a nice day."

Slowly Eclipse lowered the headset and let it dangle for just a moment before dropping it back into the cradle.

Amanda sat there looking between them, her mouth still agape. "Who are you guys?"

"That would depend on your next action, sister." The Drifter leaned forward over her desk. "We can either be your best friend or your worst nightmare. Which do you choose?"

Amanda glanced toward Eclipse one more time before her shoulders gave a defeated slouch. "What do you need me to find?"

The Drifter sat back in the chair, folding his arms over his chest again. This time he also crossed a knee casually over his other leg. "We're looking for a boy. He's on this world, but not this time. We need to know which time period he is in."

Amanda looked at them like they had lost their minds. "I've never looked for anything in another time. I'm not sure I can. If someone referred you to me, then they obviously don't know me that well. You might be wasting your time."

"Ah, came highly recommended, believe me. I'll take that chance that I'm not wasting my time. I need you to try. Just because you've never done that before doesn't mean it's impossible. It just means that you haven't been given proper incentive." The Drifter smiled, a little wag going through his shoulders as he settled back into the chair. "But as you can see, my friend here can be very persuasive."

Amanda rose from her chair. "I need to get something from my car. I don't keep those things in my office for obvious reasons."

As she hurried around the desk and went for the door, Eclipse followed her. He wanted to be able to see where she was going, which car she was getting into. Thoughts of running away raced through her mind. As she reached the door, he felt he better offer her one more incentive to stay. "Amanda, one more thing…"

As Amanda turned to look at him, Eclipse extended his wings. Her eyes widened in horror.

"I fully expect you to return shortly," Eclipse threatened, "because if you don't, I will still be able to find you."

"What are you? No, never mind." Amanda gave a

terrified nod as she quickly headed out to her car. Eclipse watched as she opened the driver-side door but she never got inside. Instead, she popped her trunk and went back to retrieve something from it. A moment later, she relocked her car and returned with a box. The small cardboard box couldn't hold much. But if she had put the oracle lifestyle behind her, she may not need much anymore. She may have gotten rid of all of her other things. Or, if she'd never had any training at all, she might not have much equipment to begin with.

Once back at her desk, Amanda opened the lid and pulled out a deck of tarot cards and a small crystal ball. She turned, picked up the sugar cookie candle, and placed it on her desk.

"So much for leaving this life behind," the Drifter teased.

She actually gave a little bit of a smile. "Sometimes I do like to know what's going to happen, what the outcome of the situation is going to be. I can't say that I never look for myself."

The Drifter nodded to Eclipse and motioned him over. "We'll need that item of the boy's?"

Eclipse pulled out his box which held Calzel's hair. He didn't open it, but placed it on the desk and slid it across to Amanda. She cast a glare at him, then reached out, dropped her hand on the box, and pulled it slowly toward her. She glanced to the Drifter as though she wanted to ask him something, but her brown eyes flicked back to Eclipse with a thread of fear and she decided not to speak.

After positioning the candle behind the crystal ball, she opened the box and took out the hair from inside. Eclipse looked at the Drifter, who gave a pleased smile and nodded back. Since the Drifter had only asked for the boy's item and Eclipse had never said that it wasn't the box, how had Amanda known that the component she needed was inside the box? As the Drifter had said, she was very talented whether she acknowledged her own power or not.

She held the hair over the flame, watching it through the crystal ball. Bumps raised on her skin down the length of her arms.

Eclipse's stomach gave a jolt as he felt her make a connection to the Humline. As the sensation trembled down him, he felt goose bumps raise on his own arms and at the nape of his neck. The flame ignited the hair, burning it all the way up to her fingertips before she released it. Eclipse felt a panic as his last remnant of the boy turned to ash, but if he didn't find the boy now, he never would. This had to work.

"You will find him in the Shanasta period," Amanda said. She exhaled a long, exclaiming sigh as she slowly and unfearfully raised her gaze to Eclipse. "And are you ever in for a surprise."

"What does that mean?" Eclipse asked.

Amanda lay her hand on top of her box of tarot cards. "Is that a request for me to pull a card for you?"

Eclipse took a step back, wondering when she'd gone from fearful to confident and thoroughly reversed their positions. Why was he suddenly scared of her and her little box of cards? It took a full moment before he felt confident enough to say, "Yes." Or was he even sure that he had made the decision of his own accord?

She grinned, a shark about to devour her prey. Flipping the lid open on her box, she withdrew the cards and began to shuffle them from one hand to another.

When the deck ran out, she changed hands and started again. A card flipped out, twisted in the air a couple of times, and landed face-down by the candle. "That one is feeling hot tonight," she commented as she reached out to pick it up. Confident and poised, she seemed like a completely different woman than they had first met.

The scent of sugar cookies wafted toward him, the warmly sweet smell trying to entice him to a memory long forgotten. An odd sensation curled in his stomach as he felt like he should know something. His skin prickled in warning and it set him on edge. He leaned forward on his feet, waiting.

Eclipse found himself holding his breath as she studied the card. She put it down on the table and tapped her index finger against it. "Knight of Swords," she announced with humor fully melting over her tone. "You are ready for a challenge. I suspect it's been a while since you've seen a worthy challenge. Be brave, my dear novihomidrak. You will find your star."

Considering that he had never told anyone about the star in the Humline's calculations or the comments to be brave, Eclipse knew that her reading had to be accurate. How else would she have known?

"Thank you," Eclipse said with genuine emotion. "Your assistance to us is appreciated."

"Of course."

The Drifter leaned over and touched her hand. Eclipse felt a surge of magic leave the Drifter and enter Amanda. "Never be afraid to use your powers."

Looking over Amanda, she seemed like she'd seen something that changed the world. He wondered what sight the Drifter had left her with as a reward for helping them. Being a scarcity within the worlds of the

Onesong, Drifters were normally the most sought after type of maege, usually allowing the Drifter's pockets to be filled with gold in the process. The generosity of a Drifter bestowing a future-sight vision was a very rare thing indeed.

Eclipse picked up his box and stored it back in his pouch. Knowing that it was empty now, it felt strangely odd to not have that tiny, minuscule weight of the boy's hair inside of it. Eclipse hoped the boy knew that he would find his way across any chaos door or time periods that the curse sent Calzel through. Eclipse would make sure this curse ended. And the time was now.

Amanda was already putting her belongings away, not in the box, but arranging them on her desk as the Drifter and Eclipse headed for the door.

"Voche ahm kotoo drenkashae," the Drifter said with a wave of his arms.

The Drifter and Eclipse went through the door which looked out into one world, but exited into another. The tall buildings Eclipse had seen on one side turned to smaller structures, usually only one or two stories rather than fifty. Concrete streets turned to dirt. The scent of smoke shrouded the air along with the fogginess that accompanied it, and a solid layer of ash seemed to lightly coat the streets and houses. A man staggered across their path, giving them a toothless grin. As his footprints lead through the ash, Eclipse realized that this was a way of life for the people of this period. He looked around and saw why. There, just down the street, were the big iron gates blockading a brick pathway which led to a crematorium. In the distance, Eclipse saw several more crematoriums all churning out streams of smoke and soot.

The Drifter raised the hood of his cloak and slumped his shoulders forward as he headed down the street. "I should've known this would be a plague time," he growled.

"A plague time?"

"There's an epidemic going on here. We landed in a time where the deaths have become numerous enough that they can no longer bury their dead. They have to burn them. They don't even bother to remove anything from the corpse, partially out of fear that they will get the disease and partially because they don't have the time to. People are dying that fast."

Being nearly immortal, Eclipse had no worries about himself. "Should I be concerned about you or the boy?" he asked.

"Wow," the Drifter said, eyeing Eclipse warily. "A novihomidrak concerned for another. Are you sure you're not sick? Maybe the plague has gotten you already."

"I don't know where you got this notion that novihomidraks don't care about people, but you should know you are wrong." Eclipse kept his tone very matter-of-fact. "Novihomidraks couldn't do what we do if we didn't care."

"Then maybe you ought to discuss tempering your attitude toward other magical humans."

While it felt like a slap and left a sting about as long-lasting, Eclipse wondered about the source of the Drifter's comment. He didn't bother to ask though. Some things were not his business. If the Drifter once had a bad encounter with a novihomidrak, then only Eclipse's behavior now could change the prior opinion.

The Drifter's footsteps got heavier as he hurried to

keep up with Eclipse's pace. Or maybe he sensed the mental wall Eclipse had put up to provide distance between them with their latest conversation. Either way, a serious contemplation had fallen over the Drifter. "Yeah," he stated flatly, "there's cause for concern. Drifters are in and out of so many dimensions that we build up a pretty solid immune system, but it doesn't mean we can't get sick. Plagues are usually the worst of the worst on a planet."

"Don't touch anything," Eclipse said.

"That's all fine and dandy if it is a communicable disease, but it might also be airborne."

Eclipse knew that, but he was really hoping the Drifter wouldn't bring it up. It made it feel like the curse of plague had already landed on them. "Then don't breathe either," Eclipse added.

"Funny," the Drifter muttered in response to Eclipse's snarky attitude. "What's even funnier is a novi-homidrak who doesn't think of future timelines."

Eclipse, knowing he'd just had a ring run around him, looked at the Drifter. "What's that mean?"

The Drifter snorted. "We just came from the future of this planet. Looked very well developed to me. How about you? Did you see any starving people? Cremation factories? Barren land? Heck, no! It was thriving and there were people everywhere. That means they cured this plague. Chances are, there's a vaccine for it."

So the Drifter was correct there. That still didn't help them find the boy now. "Getting to him before he's infected would be nice," Eclipse retorted.

"That we can agree on." The Drifter took the walking stick in both hands and leaned forward into it. "How about you get to work on that?"

Eclipse focused on the Humline and found it erratic and disjointed. "There's a lot of chaos energy here," he stated.

"It's a plague. What do you expect?" The Drifter threw his arms wide.

What indeed had he expected? Eclipse flinched at the question he put to himself and the little corresponding bump it caused in the Humline. But something else was off too and Eclipse found himself looking at the Drifter. The aura surrounding the Drifter had changed and sparks came off him. Eclipse noticed the Drifter clinging onto his walking stick with both hands, knuckles whitened with exertion. "Are you certain you are all right?"

The Drifter nodded, but he gave a phlegmy cough. He first covered his mouth with his fist, then rapped it against his chest as the fit ended. "Fine, fine. Any idea which direction to go?"

"We'll head this way," Eclipse said as he started down the street. Maybe he'd have a better feel for what was going on as they walked.

The Drifter grunted and followed. Eclipse couldn't help but notice how much the man leaned on his walking stick. His aura crackled more and more with each step. Eclipse let the Drifter catch up, then get slightly ahead of him. With a blink, Eclipse brought down the dragonlids and looked at the Drifter with the dragon vision. The Drifter's aura not only snapped, but it looked like lightning trying to retreat back from where they had come.

As they reached the intersection of the dirt road, the Drifter had sweat running down his face. He had even pulled off his hood. The lightning fought to go to the right now. It seemed to try to pull the Drifter in that direction. "Let's go this way," Eclipse said, indicating the street off to the left. He knew he was running on an entirely unfounded theory, but as he watched the Drifter get slower and slower while the lightning tried to flee him, Eclipse felt he might be on the correct path.

The street they took held many of the sick. People stood on the block, several of them just watching them go by with their wide eyes. Some sat on the ground. Others lay stretched out. One man even had his arms crossed over his chest. Eclipse wondered if the man knew it was his time, lay down to prepare for the end, and was dead already. Sores caked around the mouths of many of them, others had open wounds oozing pus out of them. Threadbare rags covered their shoulders. Gaunt faces turned to follow Eclipse's stride. A woman reached out from the crowd, a pleading moan leaving her lips.

Eclipse felt their misery. He reminded himself that this was not his world, or even his dimension, the latter being more important than the former. Still, he had to wonder if another novihomidrak was coming to help this world which so earnestly needed help from the chaos energy plaguing it.

He received an answer that he didn't want to hear: no help would be coming. This planet was doomed to die.

Except that, as the Drifter had reminded him, he'd just come from the future and knew that the people of this time survived the epidemic and carried on to become an advanced civilization.

Or did they?

Eclipse hated the way the Humline seemed to giggle

in his mind. How dare it try to play games with him?

He stepped in a puddle of stale water, or he hoped it was stale water, and it saturated the bottom of his robes. Eclipse chided himself for the mental slip. He'd been angry with the Humline instead of respecting that it controlled the whole flow of the world. If it wanted to play games with him, who was he to say otherwise. After all, he was merely a speck of the Onesong's energy here playing the part as a savior of the world. Didn't he sometimes make jokes with himself? Wouldn't the universe like to have joyful little experiences too, maybe have a good laugh at itself while playing a role every now and then?

The Drifter, on the other hand, was a growing concern. His pace slowed and sweat now dripped off his head. Eclipse couldn't see that it appeared to be like any of the symptoms the people on the street had, but maybe these were the early signs.

It would take a long time to get home if something happened to the Drifter. In that time, Eclipse could lose the boy to the plague.

"Do you want me to go ahead and search for him?" Eclipse asked.

"Impatient now, are you?" the Drifter grunted between gasping breaths. "I must go with you."

Now Eclipse did feel impatient. Why did the Drifter have to go with him? There was absolutely no indication of a dire need for the Drifter to be right beside him at all times from the Humline.

Keeping himself in check for the slow pace the Drifter now traveled at, Eclipse glanced around. Filth ran in streams through the streets. Dirty children played with sticks and rocks in the middle of the road, dancing in and around the rivulets as they went. Eclipse found himself looking to the sky and wondering how often it rained here. This poor city certainly needed a good deluge right now to wash it and its people. He wondered if the children played in the rain or if they went running for cover.

He thought about the unlucky boy who had been drenched under the tree on the stormy day that Eclipse had found Calzel. Somehow, he had a feeling that the stable boy would rather have been out playing with these children than taking care of pigs and chickens, especially in the rain.

Of course, how many of these kids would fall sick and die?

As he asked himself the question, a man pushing a cart full of corpses walked by. A hand dropped out over the side and Eclipse realized it was the hand of a boy not yet in his teens. Eclipse nudged the Drifter's arm as he turned to follow the cart. Instinct told him to follow the cart. There was too much of a coincidence in his thinking for this to be anything but synchronicity.

If nothing else, he still knew how to trust his gut when listening to the Humline. He wasn't yet that old.

The sound of the cart's wheels changed as the man shoved it up over the small ridge between dirt and walkway and began to roll it over the bricks leading to the crematorium.

"Hey, hey, hey! Get out of here." The man hauling the cart dropped it onto its single leg on the backend. At first, Eclipse thought the man was talking to him, but the man walked right on by him and headed over to another who looked as if he wielded a tripod camera. "We don't need any of that here."

Since the Drifter already had momentum going, Eclipse continued his stride down the brick road. He certainly didn't want to draw the attention of the man who been pushing the cart.

"Are you going to record all the names of the dead?" The man with the camera asked the man who had been hauling the cart. "All of these people are dead, aren't they?"

"I don't need any of this. I'm just doing my job."

"Does your job include murder of those not yet dead?"

The cart hauler snatched a stick from beneath several bodies and swung it at the man with the camera, who ducked. His camera slipped from his hand, but he slid his foot out to catch it before it hit the brick. Silvery black powder sifted out of the camera onto the path. The man grabbed his equipment up and skittered off down the street.

Eclipse saw the cart hauler come back, slide the stick back under the bodies so that the end stuck out within easy reach, and lift the handles again. As Eclipse tried to get the Drifter to move faster, he looked toward the doors of the crematorium. The numbers caught his attention. 5402, the numbers on the building read. Shortly beyond that was a marking implanted in the wall. It was a star.

Star 5402.

Eclipse's breath caught. He was at the right place.

Eclipse spun as he looked around for the boy. Where was Calzel? He was certain that the boy had to be somewhere close by. A bright flash reflected off the walls of the crematorium. Eclipse turned, hands out to his side with his fingers curled as if ready for an attack. It took a moment to realize the sudden light was just the photographer's flash going off.

"Stupid news reporters. Now what are you doing here? You're not one of them too, are you?" the cart hauler asked Eclipse.

"No. We are just looking for someone." Eclipse continued to look around wishing he could use his dragon vision, but the man was standing too close to him. Eclipse couldn't risk identifying himself as otherworldly to this native.

The cart hauler grunted and continued around Eclipse. "There isn't anyone alive around here, so you best be moving on."

"Are you sure he is here?" the Drifter asked.

"There." Eclipse pointed to the building

The Drifter shaded his eyes, and then he reached out to point toward the numbers beside the star. "What? Those numbers up there? Those indicate that you'll find him here?" The disbelief in the Drifter's tone slid toward disappointment. It looked like the Drifter might say something more when a flash reflected off the star and the numbers, making them go from gold to red for an instant. The Drifter's next statement fell away.

As the cart passed him, Eclipse saw the child's hand twitch. The Humline vibrated in reply. Eclipse grabbed onto the boy's arm and fingers grasped him back.

The cart jerked in response to Eclipse tugging on the boy. The cart hauler turned and once again dropped the handles. "What do you think you're doing?"

Eclipse no longer cared if this was a native of the planet. He blinked, letting his eyes turned red and allowing his dragon teeth to extend . "You're not getting this boy," Eclipse growled.

The cart hauler stepped away. "That's right. I'm not taking the boy. Maybe the others. But not him. I get paid by the body, but not for his. You can have him."

Eclipse pulled on the boy until his upper torso started to reveal itself, then he reached his arms under and heaved the boy out. It was Calzel.

The boy groaned, but his eyes were still closed. Eclipse wondered how long Calzel been unconscious for. It may have been quite a while. Maybe he'd fallen unconscious shortly after arriving here. Time travel was never easy.

Eclipse's senses flared. They'd been found.

Cradling the boy to him, Eclipse turned and crouched down as a sword appeared and crashed down onto his back. Eclipse let Calzel slide down over his legs and set the boy down on the bricks. The novihomidrak found his weapons as he spun around, straightening up with the gauntlet on one hand and the sword in his other.

The barbarian novihomidrak leaned in for a second attack.

Eclipse caught the dull iron sword against his blade. He felt the weaker metal of the barbarian's weapon give way. Once the other novihomidrak stepped in closer, Eclipse punched him with the spiked gauntlet. The novihomidrak staggered backwards.

"Won't let put back together," the barbarian shouted. He raised his hands over his head and rushed forward. Eclipse sidestepped the novihomidrak's down thrust.

"Is this curse your doing?" Eclipse shouted.

"Won't let together."

Eclipse slashed his sword sideways, going right across

the barbarian's midriff. Blood splattered against the man's matted beard. The barbarian managed a couple more steps before dropping to his knees, then falling forward onto his face. Blood ran out over the bricks.

The cart hauler rushed over. "Can I take him? Make up for the one you took? I mean the one I let you have?"

Eclipse hissed at the mortal, who threw his hands up in the air and backed away. Eclipse watched the man go back to the cart, never looking away until the hauler picked up his cart and continued on toward the crematorium. Only then did Eclipse return his attention to the barbarian novihomidrak lying dead on the walkway. With a gust of fiery dragon breath, Eclipse incinerated the novihomidrak. Better here than with those dead from the plague in the furnaces. Still, it saddened him to know he'd taken the life of another novihomidrak.

The Drifter bent over and looked closer at the boy. A smile came to the Drifter's lips. "Yes, this is the face I remember. I've found him." Tears glistened in the old man's eyes.

"The face you remember?" Eclipse knew the Drifter had never seen Calzel and so could not know what the boy looked like. Why was the Drifter so sure this was the boy they were looking for?

The Drifter dropped to his knees beside the boy. He reached out and took Calzel's hand. "Thank you, Eclipse. I hope I can make a great king for you."

Before Eclipse could question the Drifter's words, a bright flash came between the boy and the Drifter. For a split second, Eclipse thought the Drifter might be taking the boy away. He wasn't quite sure how to defend against that. How would he be able to track the Drifter down, let alone get home, without the Drifter's help. But even before he could finish these thoughts and make a plan, the light died away and in its place sat a boy just a few years older than Calzel had been. He looked just like an older Calzel. The Drifter, however, was gone.

The teenage Calzel issued another moan, blinking his eyes open as he did. "That was some trap," Calzel said. "I couldn't have done it without you."

"What happened?"

"In my teens, I was cursed by the novihomidrak after he found a way off of the world my parents had abandoned him on."

"The barbarian?" Eclipse asked, indicating the charred spot on the walkway.

"The very same. The novihomidrak had mercilessly killed several villages on my world. My parents had been sent to stop him. They thought they'd left him on a lifeless world. He found a way to open the Wells and return. He separated the Drifter in me from the essence which makes me a Watcher of Worlds. The Drifter aged faster, while the Watcher became younger." The boy sat up as he explained. His limbs moved awkwardly as if he hadn't used them in several years. "Whenever my younger self went through a door, I was transferred to another dimension."

"So now the curse is lifted?"

"Thanks to you, it is. And the novihomidrak will never hurt me again. I owe you a great debt." Calzel got to his feet. "I knew you would be part of my destiny when I saw you through the doorway."

"Can we go home for now, my doorway prince?" Eclipse asked with a bow.

"Yes, let us do that. We have much to discuss."

READY FOR ANOTHER QUEST?

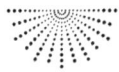

Sign up for Dawn Blair's newsletter to learn about new releases, get access to fun and free stuff, hear about events, and more!

It's easy.

Go to **www.dawnblair.com/newsletter** to join the adventure.

SPACE IS A LARGE PLACE

It needs all the champions it can get.

Even ninjas.

Amanda's adventure has just begun.

Find out what happens next in
Ninjas: By the Numbers.

https://www.morningskystudios.net/ninjas

Dawn Blair grew up on a ranch in a rural Nevada town. The old buildings provided inspiration for her imagination as she thrived on stories of unicorns, princesses, heroic knights, and hidden doors to other dimensions.

For as long as she can remember, Dawn has had a passion for storytelling. Though she started out writing, her creative life expanded into painting and illustration.

She loves creating worlds and spinning tales for people to enjoy. The best ones are the stories that surprise her as she's writing. She loves her characters doing the unexpected. She'll gladly tell you that the most exciting part about being a writer is being the first one on the journey.

Thank you for taking the time to join her on these adventures.

Find more about Dawn and read free fiction on her blog at:
www.toursofimagination.com

facebook.com/dawnblairbooks

twitter.com/dawnblair